Favourite
Irish
Legends

Best loved tales
from Ireland

GILL BOOKS

Contents

FAVOURITE
IRISH
Legends

Gill Books
Hume Avenue, Park West, Dublin 12

www.gillbooks.ie

Gill Books is an imprint of M.H. Gill & Co.

Copyright © Teapot Press Ltd 2011

ISBN 978 07171 4837 0

This book was created and produced by Teapot Press Ltd

Written by Yvonne Carroll,
Fiona Waters and Felicity Trotman
Illustrated by Lucy Su, Kay Dixey,
Robin Lawrie, Gilly Marklew
& Jacqueline East
Produced by Tony Potter
Designed by Alyssa Peacock

Printed in Europe

This book is typeset in Optima and Humanist

A CIP catalogue record for this book is available
from the British Library.

5 4 3

INTRODUCTION

This selection of the best-loved Irish legends are enjoyed by children from generation to generation. The stories will fire the imagination of readers young and old. They have been told for hundreds of years and are part of Irish history.

There are entertaining stories of leprechauns and cluricaunes. Tradition has it that leprechauns and cluricaunes are mischievous little people, often cobblers, who have pots of gold hidden away. The humans are always keen to find the gold, of course, but somehow are always outwitted by the little people's cunning and magical powers.

Learn about the great heroes of Irish history, from the stirring story of how Setanta came to be known as the Hound of Culann to the extraordinary saga of Brian Boru who defeated the Vikings at the Battle of Clontarf.

With stories of great giants, brave warriors, jealous queens and mystical creatures, there is something for everyone to enjoy.

Fionn *and the* Dragon

Fionn said goodbye to Finnéigeas and set off. The road to Tara was busy with people arriving for the great festival of Samhain. Fionn arrived in time for the feast but there was no seat for him in the banqueting hall.

"Who are you?" the High King asked,
    "I don't recognise you. Tell me your name."

"I am Fionn, the son of Cumhall," said the
young man. There was silence in the great hall.
    All eyes were on Goll Mac Morna, the man
    who had killed Fionn's father, Cumhall.
    The king spoke.

"You are the son of a friend and you are
    welcome to my feast." He put Fionn next
        to his own son and the feast began.

During the feast the High King spoke.

"For the past nine years Tara has been visited by an evil spirit. This spirit appears in the form of a fire-breathing dragon which causes great damage.

My magicians are powerless. Many warriors have tried to kill it but all have failed. Is there anyone among you who will save Tara?" the High King asked. No one spoke. Fionn stood up.

"What reward will be given to the person who is successful?" he asked.

"I will grant you whatever you want," replied the king.

"In that case I will defend Tara from the evil spirit," said Fionn.

Fionn walked to the outer walls of the city.
The sky was dark and there was no sound to
be heard. The people were gathered safely
inside the walls. Fionn heard footsteps.

"Who goes there?" he called.

"I am a friend," came the reply.

"I was a friend of your father's and I have come
to repay a favour your father did for me. As you
know, when the dragon approaches he plays
sweet music. Anyone who hears this music falls
asleep at once. Take this magic spear and as soon
as the music begins press it against your forehead
and the music will have no power over you.
I must hurry away now."

Fionn was left alone.

From the darkness came a low, sweet sound.
It was the magic music of the Fairyworld.
Immediately Fionn put the spear to his forehead
and although the people of Tara fell into a deep
sleep Fionn remained awake.

The dragon breathed a long blue flame. Fionn
aimed and fired the spear. The dragon fell dead
on the spot. Fionn cut off its head.

"What is your wish?" the High King asked.

"I ask to be leader of the Fianna as my father was," replied the proud hero. The High King agreed.

"You have a choice to make," the High King said to Goll Mac Morna. "You can accept Fionn as your leader or you must leave Ireland."

Goll thought for a while and then spoke to Fionn.

"Here is my hand. I will gladly serve you."

Once Goll Mac Morna had submitted, the other warriors of the Fianna followed. So Fionn became their leader, as his father before him had been.

The *Brown Bull* of *Cooley*

Queen Maeve and her husband, Ailill, ruled Connacht. One night they began to boast to each other about their riches and possessions. Maeve had many beautiful jewels, but so had Ailill. Ailill had fine clothes, but so had Maeve. On and on they went, comparing their chariots,

flocks of sheep and great herds of cattle. Anything that was mentioned by one was soon matched by the other. Then Ailill remembered his white bull Finnbhennach. Maeve was silent because she had no bull in her herds like this one.

Maeve sent for her druid, immediately!

"Tell me," she demanded, "where in Ireland will I find a bull as fine as Ailill's?"

"The bull you are looking for is in Ulster," replied the wise man. "He belongs to Daire Mac Fiachra in Cooley."

Maeve sent messengers to Cooley at once, to ask for the loan of the great bull for a year. In return, she promised Daire a gift of fifty heifers. Daire was delighted to help Maeve and ordered a feast to be prepared for the messengers before they returned to Connacht.

During the feast, however, one of the messengers boasted that if Daire had not given the bull willingly they would have taken it by force. When Daire heard this he was furious.

"Return to Connacht and tell your queen that she will not have my bull," he shouted as he sent the messengers on their way.

Maeve was determined to capture the bull. She assembled a great army and marched to Ulster.

It was winter time and during the winter the army of Ulster lay in a deep sleep, under the spell of the sea-witch. When Maeve's army arrived there was only Cú Chulainn and the boys of the Red Branch to defend Ulster.

Cú Chulainn made an agreement with Maeve that she would send one hero to fight him each day.

Day after day the fight continued, and each day Cú Chulainn won.

One evening, he called the boys of the Red Branch and asked them to defend Ulster. Then he lay down and fell into a deep sleep. Maeve decided that this was the time to attack. While the battle raged, she sent some of her men to capture the bull.

Cú Chulainn woke to find that most of the Red Branch boys had been killed.

By now, spring had returned and the spell of the sea-witch lifted. The men of Ulster rushed to fight but Queen Maeve retreated, driving the huge brown bull before her.

When she arrived at the castle she ordered
that the bull be put into a pen to keep him safe.
When Ailill's bull, Finnbhennach, heard the
brown bull bellowing, it charged. But the brown
bull impaled Finnbhennach on its horns and
the white bull was killed instantly. Then the bull
turned and, raging and bellowing, it thundered
home to Cooley. But, no sooner had it arrived
home, than its heart burst and it collapsed and
died. So, in the end, although a battle had
been fought, neither Maeve nor Ailill
was richer than the other.

The **Fairy Lios**

One afternoon in early summer, Eithne and her brother Connor were playing in the field behind their house. Eithne was busy making daisy chains and then she decided to pick some of the wild flowers that were growing in the field. Her favourites were the bluebells.

"Don't pick the flowers from the fairy lios, Eithne, or you will be sorry," Connor warned.

Eithne ignored his warning and continued to pick bluebells from the centre of the lios.

"There are so many growing here that the fairies couldn't possibly notice if a few were picked," she answered.

The children returned home and Eithne put the bluebells in a vase on the kitchen table. As soon as their mother heard that she had picked them from the lios, she rushed outside and put them on the window ledge. She knew that if the fairy people were angry Eithne might be punished for interfering with the lios. And so she was!

When Eithne lay down in bed that night she
jumped up screaming. Her bed was full of
nettles! She tried to sleep in her parents' bed,
but as soon as she lay down it too was full
of stinging nettles. She tried Connor's bed
but the same thing happened.

"I'm sorry I ever went near the lios," she cried.

Her parents went to visit a wise old woman
who lived nearby to ask what they should do.

"The fairies will not be easy to please," she said.

"But if someone in your family could do
a good deed for them, perhaps they might
remove the nettles."

The family thought and thought but what could
they possibly do for the fairy people? At last,
Connor had an idea. That night, he crept out
of the house and went to the lios.

At midnight the lights twinkled in the lios and he
could hear soft, light music. Connor loved music
and he could play all sorts of tunes on his feadóg
(tin whistle). He recognised some of these
tunes and thought to himself that it was
strange that the little people should
have the same music as mortals.

Cautiously, he pulled back the bushes and there in front of him were fairies and leprechauns dancing merrily!

"The leprechaun has a whistle just like mine," he thought. When the music stopped Connor moved forward. There was silence, then one of the leprechauns spoke angrily.

"Your sister disturbed our lios and now you have come to disturb our dance."

"No, no," said Connor. "I have come to tell you how sorry she is. I promise that she will never do such a thing again. Please take the nettles from her bed and let her sleep."

"Impossible!" said the leprechaun.

"Go away before we punish you too." He turned to the musician.

"Let the music start again!"

Connor stood outside the lios feeling very sad. It seemed that there was nothing to be done. His sister would never be able to sleep in a bed again. Then he had another idea.

Connor listened to the music once more. When the next dance was over and he thought that the piper was resting, he began to play a soft, sad tune. Playing his tune all the while, he parted the bushes and stepped into the lios. This time the fairy people listened.

He played for what seemed to be forever and, when he finished, not a sound was to be heard. Then the applause began and the leprechaun who had spoken earlier spoke again.

"Well played, Connor. You are a brave young man. We must reward you."

"Oh no, I don't want anything for myself. I just want help for my sister Eithne."

The leprechaun turned to the others. They nodded.

"Return home now," he said. "We will grant your wish."

Dawn broke and in an instant the lios was emptied as the Sidhe vanished.

When Connor returned home he found Eithne fast asleep in bed. His family knew that Connor had somehow broken the spell but they also knew that they could never ask how.

Paddy and the Phouka

Paddy loved stories about the fairy folk!
He especially enjoyed stories about phoukas,
who played jokes on people. They
could be fierce and frightening,
or kind and helpful.

One day, while looking after his
father's cows, Paddy felt a strange
wind, and knew it was a phouka,
going to where the fairies danced.

"Phouka," he called out. "Let me
see you! You can have my coat to
keep warm!"

Suddenly a big young bull charged at Paddy!
He threw his coat on the animal. The bull stopped
and said in a man's voice,

"Go to the mill tonight when the moon is full,
and you'll have good luck!"

That night, Paddy went to the mill. There were
sacks of corn lying around, but the men who
worked there were asleep. It was so late that
Paddy was tired and went to sleep too – and
when he woke in the morning, the corn had all
been ground into flour. This was very strange,
because all the men were still sleeping soundly.

For several nights the same thing happened. Paddy
decided he must stay awake and see how the corn
was ground! So he crept into an old chest that
he found in the mill. The chest had a big
keyhole, and he could peep out of it.

That night, looking through the
keyhole, he spied six little men
coming in, each carrying a sack
of corn on his back. They were
followed by an old man, wearing
torn and ragged clothes. The
old man set the little people to
work, and soon all the corn
was ground.

Paddy knew the old man was the phouka
he had met, with six little phoukas.
In the morning, Paddy told his
father what he had seen.

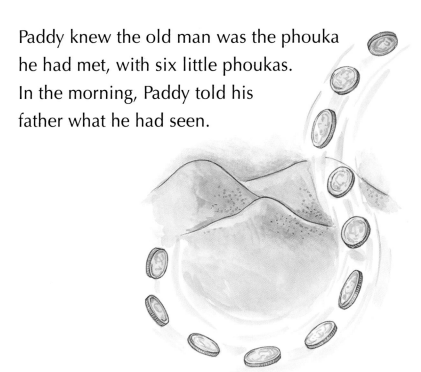

"If the phouka wants to work, I won't stop him,"
his father said, "but I will sack the lazy men
who have done nothing."

Paddy's father soon became very rich, because he
had plenty of flour to sell and no men to pay. He
never said a word about the phouka, though, for
speaking about a fairy gift would have brought
very bad luck.

Paddy often hid in the chest to watch the phoukas. He felt sad that the old man, who worked so hard keeping the little ones in order and making them work, only had tattered rags to wear. So he saved up his pocket money until he had enough to buy a splendid suit of clothes which would keep the old phouka warm in the cold mill. One night, before climbing into the old chest, he laid the clothes on the floor where the phouka usually stood.

When the old fairy came in, he saw the garments and was amazed.

"What's this? Are these for me?" he asked. "I shall be a fine gentleman."

The phouka put the suit on – there was even a silk waistcoat! – and paraded about in it. Then he looked at the corn, waiting to be ground.

"No more work for me!" he cried.

"I'm a gentleman now, and too grand to grind corn. I'm going on my travels!"

He kicked his old rags into the corner, and disappeared into the darkness.

No corn was ground that night – or ever again, because all the little phoukas ran away. But Paddy's father had made enough money to keep his family in comfort – and when Paddy himself got married, some years later, a gold cup, full of wine, appeared at his place on the table. Paddy knew the cup was a present from the phouka, and his family kept it as a treasure ever after.

The *Salmon* of *Knowledge*

Long ago in Ireland the king had a special army of soldiers called the Fianna to guard him. Cumhall was their most famous leader. His enemies were jealous of him, so they killed him. Cumhall's wife was afraid that her young son Fionn might also be killed. So she took him to two women warriors who lived on the slopes of the Sliabh Bloom

Mountains. She asked the women to teach the young boy all that a son of Cumhall should know, for she knew that one day her son would become one of the Fianna.

At that time, any youth wishing to join the
Fianna had to pass very difficult tests. He had
to defend himself against the spears of nine
men using only a shield; he had to jump
over a pole as high as his head; and he had
to recite twelve books of poetry. When
the women had taught Fionn all the fighting

skills he would need, they
sent him to Finnéigeas the
poet to learn the twelve
books of poetry.

Finnéigeas lived on the banks of the river Boyne. He had spent many years living beside the river and fishing in it. There was a fish in the Boyne known as the Salmon of Knowledge. The person who caught and ate it would know everything there was to know in the world. Finnéigeas liked the young fair-haired Fionn and agreed to become his teacher. One day as Fionn was learning poetry he heard a shout. He rushed to the river and there stood Finnéigeas holding a large salmon.

"Take the fish and cook it for me, please, Fionn," he said. "Remember you must not eat any of it."

Fionn did as he was told. He cleaned the salmon,
lit the fire and put the salmon over the fire to
cook. All was well until a blister rose on the side
of the salmon. Without thinking, Fionn reached
out and broke the skin of the blister.

In doing so he burnt his thumb and sucked it
to stop the pain. He finished cooking the fish
as Finnéigeas returned.

The old man looked at Fionn and saw
in his eyes the knowledge he had spent
so many years searching for.

"There is nothing for me to teach
you now," he said sadly.

"You must go to Tara
and take your father's
place at the head of the
Fianna. Always use your
knowledge wisely."

Fionn set off at once
to join the Fianna. From
then on, whenever he had a
problem, all he had to do was
to put his thumb in his mouth
and he had the answer at once.

Brendan the Navigator

Not for nothing was Brendan called 'The Navigator', but this latest adventure was his bravest yet. Brendan was planning to travel to the 'Promised Land of the Saints'. It was not certain that this land was real, but Brendan was determined to look for it.

The journey would be long and dangerous and Brendan was already an old man. In fact he was nearly 85 so it was small wonder that his back ached! Most of his fellow monks considered him mad. Now he went slowly into the shelter of the monastery and joined the rest of the monks for what was to be his last meal on dry land – for a very long time indeed!

The following morning dawned clear and cold:
ideal sailing conditions. After a simple meal
of porridge, Brendan and his crew walked to
the shore, and, with a blessing from the Abbot,
launched the currach. It seemed a frail craft for
such a long voyage ahead, but Brendan smiled
confidently as he took his place on board.

As they sailed away, he watched the coastline of Ireland grow smaller and smaller. At last all he could see around was the great empty sea. For many days no land was sighted; food and water became short. Brendan and the monks sometimes caught fish but they were relieved when they finally saw land, far away on the horizon. As they drew nearer, they saw an island, covered in hundreds of sheep. Brendan kept a diary of his voyage and, that night, when he wrote his usual report, he called the place the Island of Sheep, the Faroe Islands.

Next morning Brendan decided they should light a fire and celebrate Mass. They found a great hill by the shore, overlooking the island and the sea, and Brendan asked the younger monks to build a fire there. As it burned merrily, Brendan prepared for the service.

Suddenly the ground began to quiver beneath their feet and the monks looked round in terror. What was happening? Could it be an earthquake? Horrified, they watched as the fire slid slowly down the hillside, towards the sea. Brendan had to move quickly out of its path. Then he looked in amazement as a huge eye appeared out of the hill. A deep voice spoke.

"Who is setting fire to my back?" it asked.

The monks all ran away, but Brendan held his ground.

"Who are you, and where are you?" he asked.

The great eye blinked and turned around in his direction as the ground heaved again. Brendan fell to his knees as the 'great hill' moved upwards. Now he saw that it was no hill – but a huge whale!

"My name is Jasconius. As you see, I am a whale," said the deep voice again.

And truly there it was. A great whale who had been peacefully sleeping by the shore, half in and half out of the water. Brendan struggled to pour water over the huge creature's back where the fire had been lit. The whale's body shook, and Brendan suddenly realised that the creature was laughing at him.

"Gentle monk, do not fear. You have not hurt me, but the warmth of your fire has woken me up."

The monks were a little ashamed as they crept back to see what had become of Brendan. They were astonished to find him sitting on the sand, calmly talking to the mighty whale.

"My friends, you have no cause to be frightened," Brendan called to them.

"See here, this noble creature has offered to pass messages to all his brethren so that we may travel safely over the seas between here and the Promised Land."

And Jasconius was as good as his word. For the rest of their voyage, whenever Brendan and his monks met any whales, all of whom would play and leap around their boat, the creatures were careful to do them no harm and to point out the safest passage.

Finally, they arrived at a beautiful island which Brendan felt sure was, at last, the 'Promised Land of the Saints'. He was weary from his travels but his heart almost burst with joy.

"My brethren, we have reached our destination! This is the Promised Land! Give thanks to God!"

Brendan led the monks in happy prayers and joyful singing.

The journey had taken seven years. Some people believe that the Promised Land was America, although it was a further nine centuries before another man made a similar voyage. His name was Christopher Columbus.

The *Beggarman*

The Fianna were preparing to set out for a day's hunting. They had camped overnight on the Hill of Howth, Binn Éadair.

"This will be a good day," said Conán Maol.

"I feel well so I will run fast. In fact, today I will run faster than anyone anywhere!"

All the Fianna laughed, because Conán was short and rather fat. Suddenly, a voice spoke. It seemed to come from a bush nearby.

"Fast? You, run fast? Rubbish! No one could outrun me."

With that, a strange-looking sight appeared
from the bushes and stood before the Fianna.
It was an old beggarman dressed in a long,
tattered coat that reached the ground.
On his feet he wore enormous boots that
were so caked with mud that he could
barely lift his feet to walk.

While this was happening, no one noticed a
ship sailing into the bay, nor had they noticed the
warrior who had jumped ashore and was striding
across the beach towards them. As he walked,
his golden helmet glistened in the sunlight and
his purple cloak blew out behind him.

The Fianna were taken by surprise.

"Welcome," said Fionn, leader of the Fianna.

But before he could say anything else, the
warrior stretched out his arm, pointed to the
Fianna and declared,

"I offer a challenge. Choose your swiftest runner
to race against me. The winner shall have the
gold, horses and chariots of Eire."

"Caoilte Mac Rónáin is our fastest runner,"
replied Fionn, "but he is away in Tara."

"The race must take place now!" said the warrior.

"In that case," replied the beggarman, "I will accept your challenge. How far had you in mind?"

"I never race less than sixty miles."

"Fine," said the beggarman, "if Fionn will give us two horses, I suggest that we ride the distance today and race back tomorrow."

The Fianna were stunned. They could not understand how Fionn was allowing this to happen.

Early next morning, the warrior woke the beggarman. He was anxious to begin the race.

"I would never dream of running this early. If you are in such a rush, you set off and I will follow you later," said the beggarman and, curling up, he fell asleep.

When he finally woke it was mid-morning. He set off to catch up with the warrior.

What a sight he was, the
tails of his long coat
flapping in the wind
behind him as he
jumped and hopped but
never ran. But it wasn't
long before he had caught
up with the warrior.

"We are halfway there now," said the beggarman.
"Have you stopped to eat yet?"

There was no answer so he raced ahead.

"Well, I am hungry and I must eat," he muttered
to himself.

The bushes around were thick with ripe, juicy
blackberries. The beggarman began to gobble
them up. When the warrior caught up with him,
his coat and face were purple with juice.

"The tails of your coat are caught up in a bush ten miles back," snarled the warrior.

"Oh dear," said the beggarman, "I mustn't lose them!" Running backwards he found them, and with three long hops caught up with the warrior.

Meanwhile, Fionn and the Fianna were waiting on the top of Binn Éadair.

"Do you see anyone coming?" they whispered.

"I can see something in the far distance," said Conán Maol.

At the sight of the beggarman the Fianna gave a great cheer of joy and relief. But as they gathered round him, they heard the fearsome roar of the warrior as he approached with his sword drawn.

He swung the sword at the beggarman; but when the Fianna looked, the warrior's head was rolling by the beggarman's side.

"Let that be a lesson to you," said the beggarman.

"It's a lucky day for you that I'm feeling generous!" With that he reached down, picked up the head and threw it back on the warrior's shoulders where it landed back to front!

"Thank you, you have saved the honour of the Fianna and I now know who you are – the prince from Tír na n-Óg, who once a year becomes human."

"I have enjoyed my time with you but now I must return to my own people," said the beggarman.

As he raised his arm to wave, he changed into a tall fair-haired prince.

As they watched, a white mist surrounded him and when it cleared he had disappeared, leaving them alone on the Hill of Howth.

The Doctor *and the* Fairy Princess

It was late at night and there was a knock at the doctor's door. When he opened it, he saw a big black coach drawn by black horses. There was a small boy on the front step.

"Please speak to my master," the boy said. The doctor put his head through the window of the coach.

"Could you come at once? My wife needs you urgently," asked the man inside.

"I'll be with you in five minutes," the doctor said.

He dressed as quickly as possible, snatched up his bag, and joined the fine gentleman in the coach.

"Sit beside me," said the gentleman, "and don't be alarmed at anything you may see."

The coach moved at great speed, heading for
Lough Neagh. When they got to the jetty, the
doctor thought they would slow down to get
on the ferry – but the coach didn't stop!

It sped right through the water, across the lough!
The doctor began to feel nervous, as he realised
what sort of a patient he had been called to help.

Soon the coach reached the far bank of Lough
Neagh. The horses did not stop galloping as their
hooves hit dry ground. When the carriage stopped
the doctor climbed out in front of a large house.

The gentleman led the doctor to a well-lit room
hung with bright silk, embroidered in gold and
silver. A fire roared in the hearth.

On a huge bed, draped in silks and linens, lay a beautiful woman.

"Thank you, doctor," she said, "for coming so quickly."

Hours later, the woman gave birth to a baby boy. The doctor wrapped him in some fine linen cloths, and placed the baby in his mother's arms. Before the tired woman went to sleep, she put her hand on his sleeve.

"Listen," she whispered. "Take care, or a spell will be put on you to make you stay. Do not eat any food, or drink any wine. Don't show any surprise, whatever you may see. And don't take more than five guineas for your fee!" "Thank you!" the doctor said. "I shall do exactly what you say."

Then the gentleman returned. With a smile, he picked up the baby boy, walked across to the fire and laid the baby down. With the shovel,

he moved all the burning coal to the front of
the hearth and put the baby on the hot stone at
the back of the fire. Then he covered the baby
completely with the hot coal! The doctor watched
in horror but he did not make a sound.

The next moment the doctor
found himself in a great hall.
A wonderful feast was laid
and many people were sitting
down, preparing to eat.

"You must be tired and
hungry," said the gentleman.
"Please join our feast."

The doctor remembered his instructions.

"Sir," he said, "I never eat or drink between
supper and breakfast. Please let me go home.
Other patients will be waiting for me."

"Certainly," the gentleman smiled,
"but I must pay you."

From his purse, he poured a stream of gold
pieces on to the table. Although this was more
money than the doctor could earn in a lifetime,

he knew he could
not accept so much.

"My fee is five guineas,"
he said, and picked up
five coins, putting them
in his own purse.

"I must go, as it must
be nearly dawn."

The gentleman laughed.

"My lady has been telling
you secrets!" he said.

"You have done well.
The coach is waiting
for you, and will take
you home safely."

Once again, the doctor journeyed rapidly across the land and through the water. At last the carriage drew up outside his own front door and there the doctor climbed out. When he pulled out his purse, he found a gold ring set with a huge diamond there too. His own name had been engraved inside the ring. He watched as the coach drove towards the rising sun.

The doctor realised that the ring was a reward from the fine gentleman himself – the fairy prince. From that day on, the fairy's gift brought him and his family all the luck, honour and riches that they could possibly want.

The *Crock* of *Gold*

It was a clear moonlit night as Tom walked home from the village. Suddenly he heard a most peculiar sound coming from the bushes ahead. His mother had warned him to ignore strange sounds at night, as this was when the fairy people appeared. Even so, Tom paused for a moment before moving closer to the bushes to see what could possibly be making the noise.

He couldn't believe his eyes! There in front of
him was a little man no bigger than Tom's hand,
with his beard tangled in the bush. He wore
brown trousers, a green waistcoat and a bright
red cap on his head and his tiny shoes were on
the ground beside him. He had something in his

hand and when Tom looked at it closely he
saw that it was an awl the size of a thimble.

"This is my lucky day!" Tom thought to himself.

"I have found a leprechaun and every leprechaun
has a pot of gold. I just have to keep him in
sight and the gold will be mine."

Tom grabbed the leprechaun. He struggled, but Tom held him tightly and untangled his beard. This made the little man angry, but Tom ignored his bad temper and whistled a merry tune.

All the while he made sure that he
kept a firm hold on the leprechaun.

"Put me down," he shouted.

"Not until you tell me where you have
hidden your crock of gold," replied Tom.

At last, when the leprechaun realised that Tom
was determined not to let him go, he said,

"Right, I give up. The gold is buried
under this bush. Now let me go."

"Oh no!" said Tom.

"I have no spade and if I go home now, how will I remember which bush is the one with the gold?"

"Why not mark the bush with your handkerchief?" suggested the leprechaun.

"Of course!" agreed Tom, "but you must promise me that you won't take the gold when I'm gone."

The leprechaun promised, so Tom put him down and set off home.

The dawn was breaking by the time Tom returned. As he approached the bushes, what a sight met his eyes! Every bush had a bright red handkerchief tied to its lowest branch.

"What a fool I was to let the leprechaun out of

my sight," he whispered sadly to himself.
"The gold will never be mine now."

Perhaps he imagined it, but as he slowly made
his way home Tom thought he could hear the
sound of laughter blowing in the wind.

Brian Boru

The Vikings were fighting the people of Ireland and Brian had spent many hours in battle. He was weary but he was determined not to show it. He was a warrior, from the tribe of Dal Cais, and a son of Cennetig who had once been King of Munster. Brian was a still a boy, with a short spear in his grubby hand. His older brother, Mahon, had succeeded Cennetig as King. But in his heart, Brian held a secret: Eimer the fortune-teller had told him that one day he would be Ireland's greatest King.

As Brian looked round, he saw the Viking charge approach. He gripped his spear tightly and looked for Mahon who was in the thick of the fighting. But this time the Vikings were too strong and the Dal Cais were forced back, even to the gates of their fort. Brian watched in mounting horror as these wild Norsemen ran through the settlement.

Next day a deep sadness hung over the ruined houses. Brian's own mother had been killed in the raid. Brian went to Mahon and told him:

"I pledge today that I will avenge the death of my mother and will not rest until these Norsemen have been driven from Ireland for ever!"

Mahon saw the cold rage in his brother's eyes and realised that, although he was still a boy, he had grown up that day.

"Bravely spoken, my brother! We will fight side by side, and I will be proud to have you with me," he cried.

Years passed with more fierce battles. Brian grew taller and stronger and braver.

Then Mahon proposed a treaty with the Vikings.

"They are too strong for us, we cannot have any more of our countrymen killed," he declared.

But Brian remembered how the Vikings had killed their mother. He would never bow to them. So he broke away from his brother and many followed him, for he was skilled in warfare and tactics. Brian waited for the chance to fight the Vikings.

At last a great battle took place in Munster between the Dal Cassians and a huge force of Viking warriors led by Ivar. Mahon was killed. Ivar's triumph was short-lived, however: as soon as Brian was declared King of Munster, he struck hard. He challenged Ivar to a fight, killed him, and became ruler of the entire region.

By now, he was ruler of almost the whole of
Ireland, except for one man: Malachy, King
of Meath. The two men were both proud and
stubborn and neither would give in at first, but
finally Malachy agreed to support Brian. It was the
year 1002 and Brian was acknowledged as High
King of all Ireland, as Eimer had predicted. He
was called Brian Borumha, Brian of the Tributes.

Brian aimed to restore peace and prosperity to
the land after many years of desperate warfare.
He ruled his warriors with a firm hand so that
farmers could once more return to the land and
school-teachers to their classrooms. He rebuilt
many of the churches that the Vikings had
destroyed. He travelled round the country in
a fine cavalcade so that everyone might see
him and give him due homage.

Brian Boru grew to be an old man. Perhaps he ruled with too strong a hand. Some of his people became unhappy and resentful. Maelmordha, King of Leinster, decided to challenge him. He sent messengers to the Vikings and to Iceland, asking for support, and in time he amassed a huge army to challenge Brian.

The Battle of Clontarf was the fiercest in all Irish history. It began on the morning of Good Friday, 23 April, in the year 1014. Back and forth the opposing forces fought, gaining here, losing there. Brian was convinced that he would win, and so it was. The Vikings were finally driven back into the sea.

Brian stayed awhile on the battlefield with only one servant; there he prayed, giving thanks for yet another successful encounter. But, unknown to him, there was still a small band of Norse warriors determined to end his rule once and for all. If they couldn't have Ireland, they would at least get rid of its troublesome king. A warrior, Brodir, from the Isle of Man, struck the fatal blow! Within hours of winning the greatest battle of his long reign, Brian lay dead.

His heartbroken warriors held a huge 'wake'
that lasted for twelve days and twelve nights.
Bards sang of his exploits; storytellers recounted
his deeds of huge courage. His body was taken
in great state to Armagh where he was finally
laid to rest.

Brian Boru was the greatest warrior
Ireland has ever seen.

Eisirt

The king was furious! His favourite poet Eisirt had just insulted him. It had happened during the feast. The king was boasting about his great strength and that he was the greatest living warrior, when he noticed the expression on Eisirt's face. He challenged him to explain.

"You are a brave warrior, but beyond the hills there are men so tall that it would take only one of them to defeat our army and kill all our people," replied Eisirt.

The king was raging and gave Eisirt only five days and five nights to prove that these giants really existed. Eisirt set off. He had a problem. If he didn't return with proof, he would

be laughed at and would probably be punished.
On the other hand, if he found these giants
they might kill him.

After some time, Eisirt reached the palace of the King of Ulster. A feast was being held in the great hall, in honour of Fergus the king.

Although he was terrified, Eisirt walked boldly up to the guard and demanded to be let in. All the guests rushed to the tiny man.

"Stay away from me, monsters!" he roared, but his voice was no louder than the squeak of a mouse.

He pointed to a dwarf (this was Conn, King Fergus's chief poet).

"I will speak to the small giant."

Conn reached down, lifted Eisirt and placed him on the table in front of King Fergus.

"Who are you, little man, and where do you come from?" asked the king.

"I am Eisirt, chief poet and wise man of my people."

"You are very welcome here," said Fergus. "You must join us, and after you have eaten you must sing for us and tell us about your home."

The king called for a seat for Eisirt and ordered food and wine for him. This was not at all easy. Where could a chair small enough be found and from what could he possibly drink? The queen provided the answer. Her golden thimble became a wine goblet and her brooch became a seat.

"Sit and enjoy yourself, poet. You have travelled far and you must be hungry and thirsty."

"I will neither drink your wine nor eat your food!" shouted Eisirt.

There was silence in the great hall. Nobody had ever spoken to the king like this before.

Suddenly the king laughed.

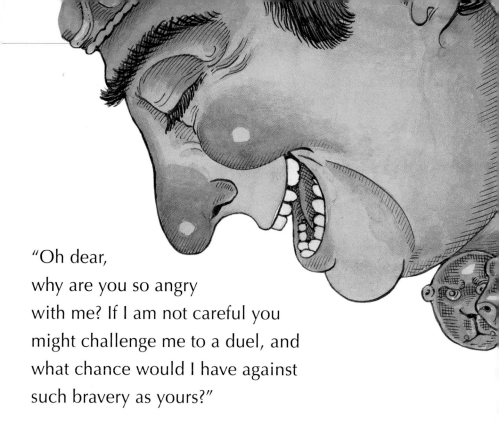

"Oh dear,
why are you so angry
with me? If I am not careful you
might challenge me to a duel, and
what chance would I have against
such bravery as yours?"

"I will put you in my goblet,
then you will have to drink!"

With that, he lifted Eisirt
and dropped him into
a goblet of wine.

The little man tried to swim.

"King Fergus of Ulster, you are doing a foolish thing. If I drown, you will never hear about my wonderful home or where it is."

"Save him! Save him!" the guests cried out.

Fergus took him out.

"Why did you insult us by refusing our kind hospitality?"

"If I told you," answered Eisirt, "you would be very angry with me. I don't think that people who make you angry live very long."

"I give you my word that I will listen to what you have to say and that you will not be harmed," answered the king.

"Well," said Eisirt, "I cannot stand injustice, and I know that you are unjust to your chief steward. I also know that he is cheating you! I cannot eat or drink here while this is happening."

There was silence in the great hall. This was treason. No one spoke to the king like this!

Then the king spoke.

"You are a strange little man with strange powers indeed. I do not understand how you know these things, for you have only just arrived in our land. You are correct. I have been unfair to my chief steward, and it must be true also that he is cheating me," said the king.

"Sir," replied Eisirt, "there is nothing worse than an unjust king, but there is nothing better than a king who admits that he is unjust and promises to change. Now I will join your feast."

Eisirt sat down, lifted the thimble and drank the wine. The guests listened long into the night as he told them wonderful stories about his people and the land from where he had come.

Soul Cages

One day Jack Dogherty met a merrow. He was wearing a red cocked hat, and was on the end of the rocks near Jack's home. Jack crossed the rocks carefully, not wanting to scare the sea fairy away.

"Good day to you, Jack," the merrow said to him.

"How do you know my name?" asked Jack, astonished.

"Your grandfather was a great friend of mine," the merrow told him. "We often used to enjoy a drink together. So of course I know who you are!"

"Where do you get drink under the sea?" asked Jack. "I thought it was all salt water."

"There are barrels and bottles in ships that sink," the merrow said. "Why don't you come and try some? Meet me here tomorrow, and I'll take you to my house!"

Jack quickly agreed, and the next day he went out to the rocks again. The merrow was there, holding two red hats.

"I've borrowed one for you," he explained. "Put this on, jump in and hold my tail."

Putting on his own hat, the merrow dived into the sea. Jack put on the other hat, jumped in, and grasped the merrow's tail. Down they went through the water, until they got to a flat, dry, sandy area. There were fishes swimming overhead, and seaweed rose up like trees. In front of them was a pretty cottage, with smoke coming out of the chimney. Inside, a splendid meal of fish was waiting for them.

Over dinner, washed down with delicious things out of the merrow's enormous collection of bottles, Jack learned that the merrow's name was Coomara, but usually he was called Coo. They talked and laughed for hours, as friends do.

One thing puzzled Jack. There were rows of wicker cages like lobster pots stacked against the walls.

"What do you keep in those?" he asked at last.

"Oh, those are soul cages," Coo told him.

"I put them out when there's a storm at sea. The souls of drowned fishermen and sailors creep into them, and then I bring them back here to keep them where it's warm and dry."

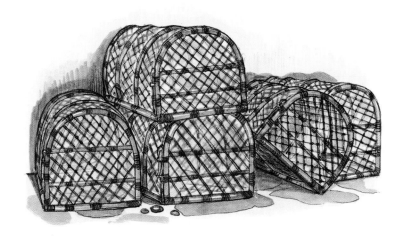

Jack peered into a couple of cages near him.
He couldn't see anything, but he could hear the
sound of crying. He felt very sorry for the souls,
shut in cages when they should be on their way
to Heaven. What could he do?

When the time came to go home, he thanked Coo very much for his great evening, and arranged to meet him out on the rocks the next day.

Back home, Jack thought hard about what he could do for the trapped souls. At last he worked out a plan. Next day, he invited Coo to come to his house. Like the merrow, Jack collected bottles that were washed up on the beach after storms and shipwrecks. That evening, when Coo came, Jack had built up a good fire, so the cabin was beautifully warm. He produced some bottles of very old, strong brandy.

Coo drank a glass while Jack only sipped at his. He poured Coo another, but soon the old merrow fell asleep by the fire.

Quickly, Jack took Coo's red hat.
He ran to the rocks, jammed
the hat on his head,
and leapt into
the sea.

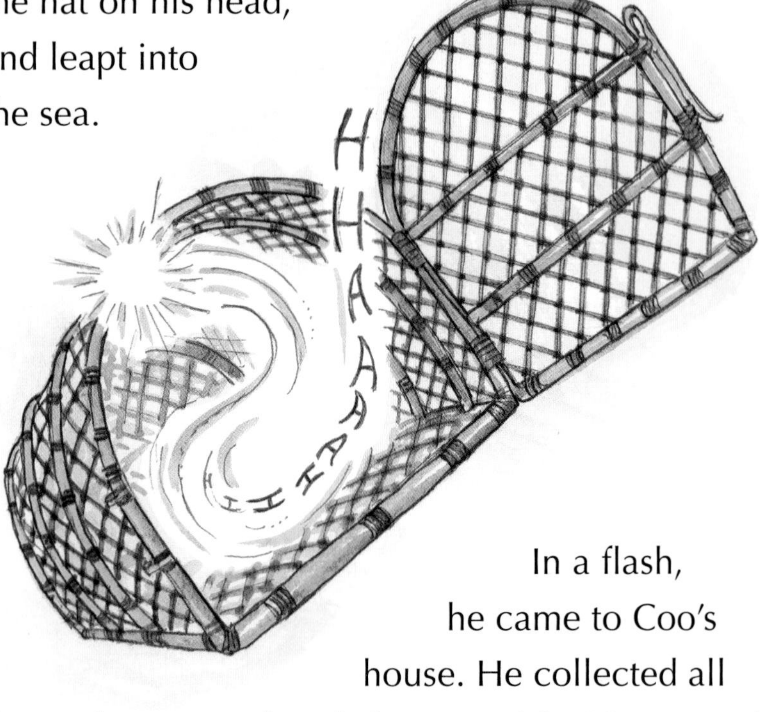

In a flash,
he came to Coo's
house. He collected all
the soul cages and took them outside. He opened
each one and shook it. There was a tiny flicker
from each cage, and a faint whistle. When every
one was empty, Jack put them back where he'd

found them. He went home to find Coo still asleep by the fire. When he woke, he thanked Jack and left. To Jack's surprise, Coo never noticed that his soul cages had been emptied! The two remained friends, and whenever there was a storm Jack would slip down to rescue any souls trapped in Coo's soul cages.

Deirdre *of the* Sorrows

When the baby Deirdre was born, her father, Feidhlim, asked the wise druids to look at the stars and tell him what the future held for her. The wise druids answered:

"This baby will cause great trouble. She will grow up to be the most beautiful woman in Ulster, but she will cause the death of many men."

When the Red Branch Knights of Ulster heard
this they were very worried for their lives.
They went to King Connor demanding that baby
Deirdre be killed. The king thought for a while.

"I have an answer," he said.

"Deirdre will be brought up far away from here
and when she is old enough I will marry her."

Deirdre was taken away at once to a deep wood.
The king chose a wise old woman, called
Leabharcham, to care for her and
teach her. As Deirdre grew older
she became as beautiful as the
druids had foretold, with long
golden hair and deep blue eyes.
But she was a very lonely girl.

One day, Deirdre told
Leabharcham about a dream
she had every night.

"I dream of a tall dark
warrior. His hair is as black
as the raven. His skin is
as white as snow. He is
fearless in battle."

Leabharcham was worried as she knew this man.

"He is Naoise, one of the Sons of Uisneach. You must never mention your dream again. You will be married to King Connor very soon," she said.

Deirdre begged Leabharcham to send for Naoise so she might meet the man of her dreams. At first Leabharcham refused but she hated to see Deirdre lonely and unhappy and finally she gave in to her request. Deirdre and Naoise met and they fell in love at once.

"We must go far away from Ulster now," said Deirdre. "I cannot marry Connor."

Deirdre, Naoise and his brothers Áinle and Ardan set off. Together they travelled all around Ireland but no one was prepared to help them because they all feared the anger of King Connor. Finally they sailed to a small island off the coast of Scotland.

There they lived for some time until one day a
messenger arrived from the king. He reported
that King Connor had forgiven them.

Deirdre did not trust the message but the
Sons of Uisneach believed it. Reluctantly,
Deirdre set off with them to Ireland.

On the way she pleaded with them to turn
back but they would not listen.

When they arrived they were sent to the
house of the Red Branch Knights,
not the king's castle. Now
Deirdre was sure that a trap
had been set for them.

Deirdre was right. Soon the house was surrounded. The Sons of Uisneach fought bravely but they were outnumbered. They were seized and brought before Connor.

"Who will kill these traitors for me?" asked the king.

None of the Red Branch Knights would kill a fellow knight. Suddenly an unknown warrior from another kingdom stepped forward.

"I will kill them," he shouted.

With one blow he cut off the heads of the Sons of Uisneach. Deirdre screamed and fell dying to the ground beside the body of Naoise. So great was her sorrow that her heart had broken.

Deirdre's father was so angry with Connor that
he left Ulster and went to live in Connacht.

Many other warriors went with him and joined the
army of Queen Maeve. This army was later to fight
bloody battles against the Red Branch Knights.

So Deirdre did bring sorrow and trouble to
Ulster just as the druids had foretold.

Niamh

Niamh sat up in bed and listened carefully. There it was again! She had heard the sounds before, but this time she decided to investigate. She slipped on her dressing gown and made her way to the bedroom door.

Down the stairs she crept. It was difficult to see because the only light to guide her was the light of the full moon that shone through the window.

Just as she reached the kitchen door she knew that she was not alone.

It was her brother Liam.

"Where are you going?" he whispered.

"I heard music again. This time I'm going to find out who is playing it. You can come with me," she replied, "but only if you do what I tell you."

Liam didn't like to be told what to do, but he was a curious little boy and the chance of an adventure was too tempting to miss.

The children stood outside in the silver moonlight and listened. The music seemed no more than a whisper or a rustling of leaves. Was it the fairy people their grandmother had told them about?

"Let's follow the path to the clearing in the wood," whispered Niamh. "I think that's where they meet."

Liam agreed and they set off into the chilly night, full of excitement – and a little frightened as well.

A faint light flickered in the bushes as they approached the clearing. They could hear music – sweet, light music. Niamh couldn't decide what instruments were playing. She thought she could hear harps and flutes. It seemed as if the music was calling her.

"Don't go too close," her brother warned.

"Gran said that if the fairy people catch you, they'll keep you. Quick, let's go home."

Niamh crept closer and closer to the light.

"Look!" she whispered excitedly. "Look! I was right all along!"

Liam peeped through the branches. What a sight it was! Lights twinkled from the trees in the clearing. The children could see little people dancing in the centre. Gran's description of the leprechauns was perfect, right down to the silver buckles on their tiny shoes.

A new dance began with a faster rhythm. The music seemed to call them to join the dance. Liam remembered his Gran's warning to cover his ears.

Niamh was spellbound. She began to move in time with the music. Suddenly there was a flash of light and Liam was blinded for a moment.

When he opened his eyes again, he was alone
and his sister had vanished. The search for Niamh
went on for a long time but there was not a
trace of her to be found.

Early one morning, many years later, Liam returned to the clearing in the wood. Although he now lived far away, he visited the spot where his sister had disappeared whenever he could.

As he approached he heard a child calling,

"Liam! Liam! Where are you? We must go home."

The voice was familiar. A little girl ran up to him and asked,

"Have you seen my brother? We were dancing with the fairies and the leprechauns for twenty minutes and he's wandered off! It's time we went home."

Liam stared at her in amazement.

"Niamh," he said, "Is it really you? You haven't spent twenty minutes dancing, you've been away for twenty years!"

Granuaile

Granuaile was the daughter of the chieftain Owen Dubhdara. She grew up in Belclare Castle, a fortified tower with a great hall where the clans would gather for huge feasts. She had been christened Gráinne. From early childhood, she loved being with her father on board one of his great fleet of ships. Her father did his best to discourage her because she was a girl, but Gráinne was determined. She cut off all her hair and borrowed some of her brother's clothes. When she appeared dressed as a boy and demanding to be taken on the next voyage, her mother was angry, but her father laughingly agreed to take her with him. And so her life on the high seas began. From then on she was known as Gráinne Mhaol, Bald Grace, and in time this name became shortened to Granuaile.

Granuaile's husband was called Donal O'Flaherty.
Her parents thought he might tame their
wild daughter, as he was known as Donal an
Chogaidh, 'Donal of the Battles'. But although
she bore three children, she became ever more
involved in the adventures of the O'Flaherty clan.
She had learnt much from her father and men
were impressed with her skill. When Donal was
killed in an ambush, Granuaile defended her
castle successfully against her husband's enemies.

Although the O'Flahertys admired Granuaile greatly, they would not accept her as their leader after Donal was killed. So Granuaile returned to her father who was very proud of his daughter's exploits. He gave her the castle on Clare Island to live in and there she set up as a chieftain in her own right, with some two hundred followers. Granuaile then turned to piracy and became the most daring and feared pirate on the west coast, her coffers overflowing with stolen treasure.

By now the English realised that she had to be stopped. She finally met her match in the new governor of Connaught, Sir Richard Bingham. He chased her on the seas, threatened to put her to death and finally imprisoned her. Two years in Dublin Castle almost destroyed her brave spirit, but she was released when she promised to give up piracy.

By now Granuaile was growing old and she decided to write to Elizabeth I, Queen of England, to ask for the Queen's protection in the future. In time the Queen replied, asking several questions. Granuaile decided to travel to London to see her.

As she waited to be received by the Queen, she began to daydream about the exciting life she had led and did not hear the Queen's servant speak.

"Madam!" he said. "I insist you accompany me to the inner chamber."

"Her Gracious Majesty Queen Elizabeth is ready to receive you."

Granuaile started back from her daydreaming. She looked down her haughty nose at the impatient courtier.

"Do not sneer at me, you popinjay," she roared. "Do not believe that I am not an important person just because I do not wear fine clothes like the Queen of England. In my lands I am as powerful as your Gracious Queen."

Granuaile brushed the courtier aside, and strode off to meet the Queen.

The two women looked each other in the eye. Each knew the other was brave and fearless.

"You are most welcome to my court," said the Queen. "Pray sit here by my side and let us talk."

Granuaile bowed her head and sat beside the Queen. They made a strange pair, both no longer young, both proud. The Queen was dressed in a beautiful dress with rings on her fingers. She wore much make-up, and a red wig covered her head. Granuaile wore no make-up, her grey hair was her own and was simply tied back with a ribbon. Her dress was of plain wool, her velvet cloak was old and worn and the only sign of her wealth was the gold brooch pinned on her shoulder.

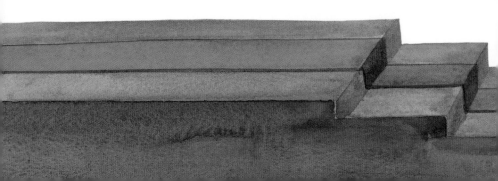

The two women talked for a long time, to the amazement of the rest of the courtiers. And when Granuaile walked out of the court that day, she held her head even higher. The Queen had granted every one of Granuaile's requests. Her brother and her son were released from prison, and she herself was provided with a living for the rest of her days.

Granuaile lived until she was in her seventies, a
good age in those times. Even as an old woman,
she remained a leader who was admired by all
her followers. And by a strange coincidence, she
died in 1603, the same year as Queen Elizabeth –
two women who, despite their very different
lives, had met and understood each other.

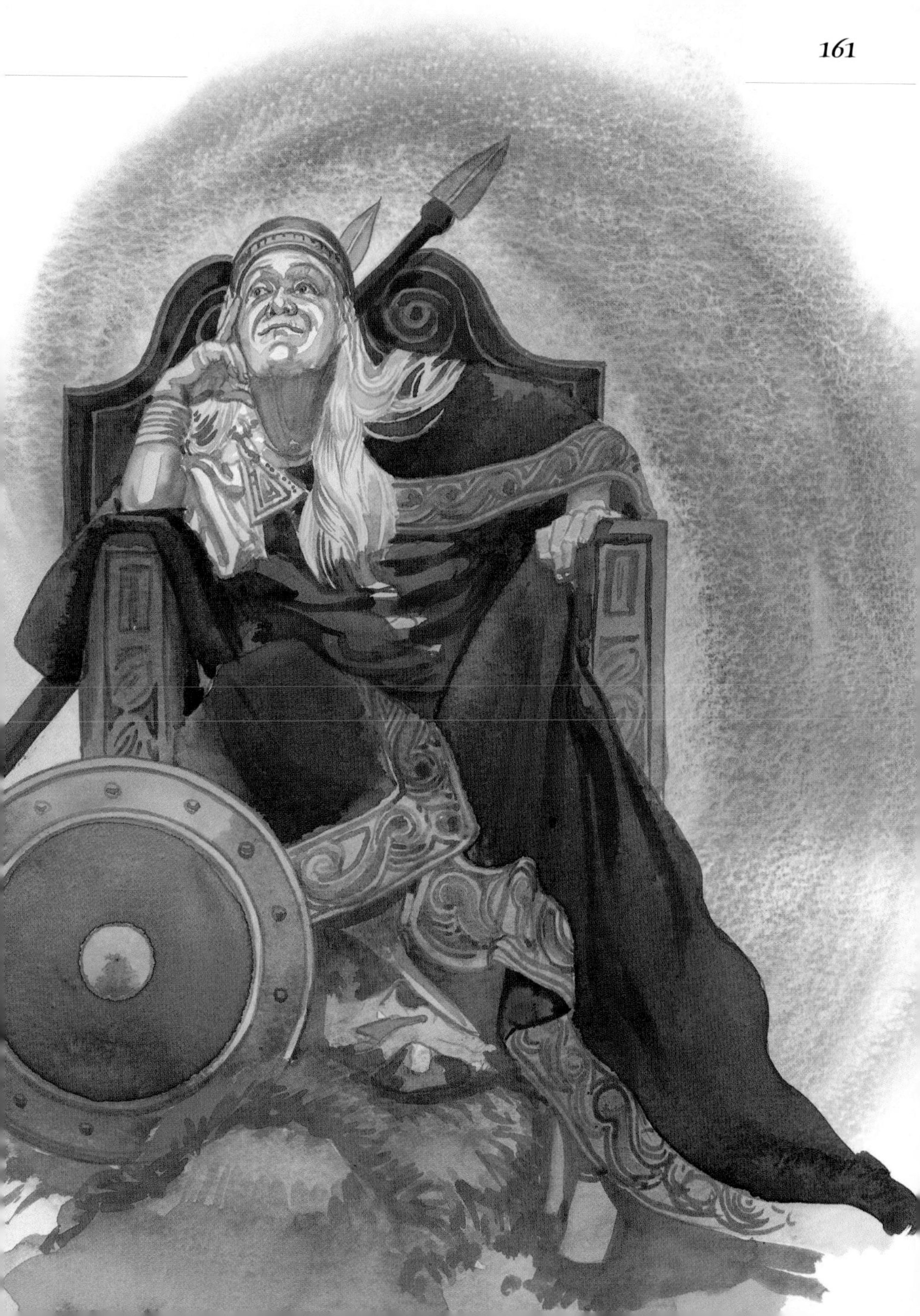

The *Giant* from **Scotland**

Fionn and his wife Una lived in their castle by the sea in County Antrim. One day a stranger arrived. It was a messenger from Scotland, a country across the sea.

"I bring a challenge from the mighty Angus," the messenger said. "He is the tallest, strongest and most fearsome giant in all Scotland. He has heard about your great strength and wants to fight you. Angus has beaten all the other giants and you are the only one remaining. Do you accept the challenge?"

"Of course I accept," said Fionn.

"I will begin to prepare immediately."

And so he did!

From that day on, Fionn worked hard. He
had decided to build a path across the sea to
Scotland. It was a rather unusual causeway
made up of hundreds of thousands of black
rocks, all different sizes and different heights.

Some rocks had six sides, some eight and others more than ten sides.

The warriors of the Fianna looked on in amazement as Fionn worked each day. Before long the causeway stretched miles into the sea. One evening when Fionn returned home he noticed that Una was worried.

"What is the matter?" he asked.

"Oh, Fionn," she replied, "I heard some very disturbing news today. I heard that Angus is indeed much bigger than you and that he is definitely stronger."

"If I cannot beat him with my strength, then we must think of a plan. I may not be as big or as strong as he is, but I am much cleverer."

Fionn and Una talked for many hours. They thought of many plans, but could not find one that they were sure would work. Time was running out.

Later that week the messenger from Angus returned and told Fionn that Angus would arrive in two days' time.

"Tell him that Fionn is ready and waiting," said Una. "Do not worry Fionn, I have a plan in mind."

Una worked hard for the next two days. She spent the time busily cutting and snipping and sewing and knitting.

"Imagine sewing and knitting at a time like this!"
Fionn exclaimed. "I thought you had a plan."

"Look carefully," said Una. "What do you see?"

Fionn was amazed.

"Clothes," he said. "I see clothes,
but they are most peculiar!"

"Never mind that," said Una, "just put them on!"

What a sight Fionn was! He wore a long dress, on his feet he had a pair of giant brogeens (booties) and Una had knitted a beautiful bonnet for his head.

"While you were working, I asked Fergus to make a very large cradle. In you get," said Una, "we have no time to lose!"

Angus was approaching. As he walked the ground shook.

"Where is the mighty Fionn? I have travelled all the way from Scotland to find him," the giant roared. "Is he afraid to meet me?"

Una opened the door.

"Please come in. You are very welcome. Fionn is hunting and won't be very long. But please sir, could you speak a little softer, our baby is asleep."

"That is your baby?" Angus gasped in shock.

"Yes he is rather small now, but he will grow," replied Una.

Angus was frightened. He had never seen a baby this big.

"If this is Fionn's small baby, what size is Fionn?" he wondered. "Fionn himself must be enormous!"

Angus hurried out and, without turning, he ran across the causeway.

As he was running a thought struck him.

"What if Fionn is following me?"

To prevent this happening, he began to remove stones from the path and, by the time he arrived home to Scotland, all that was left was a few yards of path jutting out from the coast of Antrim into the sea. To this day, only that part of the causeway remains.

Seeing is Believing

Felix O'Driscoll was a noisy young man, who loved to swagger about and joke with his friends. He often boasted that he didn't believe in fairies, ghosts and cluricaunes. Nonetheless, he did sometimes feel a little nervous at night and when he rode past the old churchyard after dark, he always made his horse trot quickly and cast anxious looks all around him.

Most evenings, Felix and his friends met in the village pub. They loved sitting down together and telling stories of fairy folk – each one tried to outdo the others' stories! Felix would laugh at these tales

and always insisted loudly that fairies didn't exist. Although his friends might not have seen any of the little people, they couldn't quite bring themselves to say they didn't believe in them.

One day, when Felix was particularly noisy as he boasted that there were no fairies, he heard a voice coming from a dark corner of the pub.

He saw an old woman wrapped in a cloak and smoking a pipe.

"Fairies and cluricaunes do exist," she declared. "I've met one myself. Seeing is believing."

Felix and his friends were intrigued. They gathered round the old woman. "Tell us what happened," they said to her.

"It was a very long time ago and I was still a young girl," began the old woman. "It was a lovely warm June day, and I was knitting in my garden, listening to the singing of the birds and watching butterflies fluttering from flower to flower. The air was fresh and sweet.

"I was keeping an eye on the bees, for they were about to swarm and were humming loudly as they flew from hive to hive. Suddenly I heard a noise! It was coming from the rows of beans in the corner of the garden, and it was a kind of tapping – tick-tack, tick-tack – just like a cobbler nailing the heel on a shoe."

"I put down my knitting, and
crept quietly up to the beans.
There in the middle was a tiny old
man. He was wearing a black hat on
his head, and a grey coat with big buttons.
His shoes had silver buckles that were so large
they almost covered his feet! He was smoking a
little pipe and hammering the heels on to a pair of
shoes. I knew at once that he was a cluricaune."

"Good day to you," I said.
"That's hot work on a warm day."

"He looked up at me crossly. I reached down and grabbed him. When I had him in my hand, I asked him for his purse of gold."

"Gold?" he said. "And where would a poor old man like me get any money?"

"None of your tricks!" I told him. "Everyone knows that each cluricaune has a magic purse – and that however often you take a coin out, there's always another coin left in the purse." I pulled a knife out of my pocket, and made the fiercest face I could at him. "Show me your purse of gold, or I'll cut the nose off your face!" I ordered.

"The little old man looked so frightened that I nearly let him go.

"All right," he said, "you'll have to come with me a couple of fields away, and I'll show you where my money is."

"We set off towards the field. As we walked I held him firmly in my hand, and didn't take my eyes off him for a second."

"All of a sudden I heard a very loud buzzing just behind me."

"Watch out!" the cluricaune shouted. "Your bees are swarming!"

"I turned my head, fool that I was, but saw nothing at all behind me. Then I looked back at the cluricaune in my hand – but my hand was empty!

I had foolishly taken my eyes off him for the briefest of moments, and he had disappeared like smoke."

"He never came near my garden again."

The old woman sat back when she finished her story. Felix and his friends looked at each other in amazement – but it seemed as if the story really must be true.

Felix certainly believed her – and never again did anyone hear him say that he didn't believe in the little people!

Setanta

Seven year old Setanta was determined to become a member of the famous Red Branch Knights of Ulster. His father, the King of Dundalk, had told him about the special school in Armagh, called the Macra, for the young boys who would one day join the brave warriors. Setanta pleaded with his parents to let him go there but they refused.

"You are much too young, Setanta. Wait just a little longer and then we will allow you to go," they said.

Setanta decided he could not wait any longer and so one day he set off for Armagh. It was a long journey but Setanta had his hurley and sliotar to play with. He hit the sliotar far ahead and ran forward to catch it on his hurley stick before it hit the ground.

When Setanta reached the castle of King Connor at Armagh, he found the hundred and fifty boys of the Macra gathered on the great plain in front of the castle. Some of them were playing hurling and as this was his favourite game he hurried over to join in. Almost at once he scored a brilliant goal.

The other boys were furious that this young boy had joined their game uninvited and they attacked him. Setanta fought bravely. The noise disturbed the king who was playing chess. He sent a servant outside to see what was happening. Setanta was brought before the king.

"I am Setanta, son of the King of Dundalk, your brother. I have come all this way to join the Macra because I want to become one of the Red Branch Knights as soon as I am old enough."

The king liked Setanta's brave words and welcomed him to the Macra.

Time passed quickly for Setanta. He loved his
new life at the Macra.

One day, Culann, the blacksmith who made
spears and swords for Connor invited
the king, his knights and Setanta to a feast.

When it was time to set off for the feast, Setanta was playing a game of hurling. He told the king that he would follow as soon as the game was finished.

The feast began and Connor forgot to mention that Setanta would be joining the party later. Thinking all his guests had arrived, the blacksmith unchained his wolfhound which guarded his house each night.

As soon as the game was over, Setanta set out.
When he arrived at Culann's house he heard
the deep growls of the wolfhound. Suddenly the
hound leapt forward out of the dark to attack.
Setanta saw the sharp teeth bared. With all his
strength Setanta hurled his sliotar down the
hound's throat. Then he caught the animal by its
hind legs and dashed it against a rock.
With a loud groan the wolfhound fell
down, dead. Inside, the feast party had
heard the dog growling.

"My nephew Setanta," Connor cried.

"I forgot about him!"

He and the Red Branch Knights rushed out
expecting to find the young boy torn to pieces.

Connor was amazed and delighted to find his
nephew alive and he was proud of his great
strength. Culann was relieved that the boy was
safe but he was sad that he had lost the wolfhound
he loved, which had faithfully guarded his house
every night.

"Let me take the place of your hound until I
have trained one of its puppies," said Setanta.

Culann agreed. From that day
on Setanta was called
Cú Chulainn which
means the Hound
of Culann.

The **King** with **Donkey's Ears**

One day, a messenger called at the home of a poor widow.

"I have been sent by the king to bring you this message. Your son is to come to meet the king tomorrow morning. The king has a very special job for him," he said.

The poor woman was very worried. Her son was a barber and once a year the king summoned a barber to cut his hair. The strange thing was that no barber had ever returned home after his visit to the king.

No one knew that the king had a terrible secret. You see, he had very strange ears and to hide them he had to have his hair cut in a very special way. In fact, his ears were just like the ears of a donkey. Every barber who had ever cut the king's hair had been put to death immediately, so that he could never reveal the king's dreadful secret.

The woman was so worried about her son that she made her way to see the king.

"My son is all that I have in the world," she cried.

"Please do not kill my son. If he dies I will have no one to care for me."

The king listened to the old woman's pleas and felt sorry for her. He sat thinking for a while and finally he spoke.

"I will agree to spare his life on one condition," he replied.

"Your son must faithfully promise never to tell any living person about anything he sees whilst he is in my castle. If he makes this pledge, his life will be spared."

Next day, the son arrived to cut the king's hair. Imagine his surprise when he saw the king's ears!

However, he was a clever boy and he knew that his life depended on his keeping the secret, so he said nothing.

As time passed his mother noticed that her
son was unwell. He could not sleep nor eat.
There seemed to be something troubling
him, but when she questioned him he
would not answer.

She decided to send for a druid.

"I cannot help him," the druid said.

"He knows a terrible secret. He has promised
not to tell any living person his secret, but
unless he tells it he will not get better."

The wise druid thought for a while.

"I have the solution to the problem. He must go into the forest and find the tall willow tree that grows beside the stream" said the druid.

"If he whispers the secret to the leaves, the promise will not be broken because he will not have told any living person."

The boy followed the advice of the wise druid and immediately he felt as if a heavy weight had been lifted from his shoulders.

That was not the end of the story. Some days later the king's harpist went into the forest to cut some wood for a new harp. He picked a tall willow tree which stood beside the stream and began to chop the wood.

That night the harpist was called before the king and the other chieftains to entertain them. As he began to pluck the strings of his new harp, a strange music filled the room.

"The king, the king, has donkey's ears, has donkey's ears," it sang.

The dreadful secret was revealed. At first the king was terrified, but when he saw that no one was afraid of him, or laughed at him, he knew that he would never have to hide his donkey's ears again.

Paying *the* Rent

Bill Doody was sitting on a rock by a beautiful lake in Killarney. It was early one lovely May morning but Bill wasn't enjoying the view over the sunlit water or listening to the birdsong. He was in despair as he thought about his wife and his four little children.

"Tomorrow the rent is due, and I haven't any money," he said to himself.

"What are we going to do? And where will we go? If I can't pay the rent, our goods will be taken and we'll all be thrown out of our house to starve."

He had seen no one around, so he got quite a fright when a tall, well-built man suddenly appeared from a clump of gorse growing by the lake's edge.

"What's the matter with you?" the man asked Bill.

Bill wondered who this man could be. Where had he come from? Was he even from this world? But he plucked up his courage to answer the man.

"My cows have given no milk, so I have no butter to sell, and if I can't pay my rent by midday tomorrow, I am going to be turned out of my farm. And then what will happen to my wife and children? I don't know what to do."

"That's a sad story," said the big man. "But if you tell it to your landlord, surely he'll not be so cruel as to turn you out?"

"You don't know my landlord!" Bill told him. "He's a hard man – and anyway, he's had his eye on my farm for a long time. He wants to give it to one of his relatives, so I know he'll do nothing to help us."

Bill's hat was lying on the ground beside him. The stranger pulled a fat purse from his pocket, opened it and began to pour a stream of gold into the hat.

"Take this!" he said. "Pay your rent, but it won't do your landlord any good. I remember better times, when I would have dealt severely with someone as greedy and unkind as that!"

Bill stared at the gold in amazement. Then he tried to bless the man and thank him but he had gone.

Bill saw him far away, riding a handsome white horse across the lake. Suddenly, he realised who it was.

"O'Donoghue!" shouted Bill. "It was the great prince O'Donoghue!" Bill knew all the stories about this ancient prince. He had been a wise and just ruler and then he had gone to live in a palace in Tír na n-Óg. Sometimes he came back from under the waters of the lake to help lost travellers and poor people.

He raced home to tell his wife Judy what had happened, and show her the gold. She couldn't believe that suddenly their luck seemed to be changing.

The next day, Bill went straight over to his landlord's house.

"Hand over your rent, Doody," the landlord snarled. "And if it's a penny short, you'll be out on your ear before nightfall!"

"Here you are," said Bill. "Please count it, and give me a receipt."

The landlord was expecting to see piles of copper coins on his desk – or maybe a few small silver ones, or a grubby banknote.

He was stunned to see gold pieces! Quickly, he counted the money – it was the exact amount.

The landlord was furious that Bill had paid up, and he had not been able to ruin him. Without speaking, he wrote out a receipt and pushed it into Bill's hand. Then he showed Bill the door and returned to his desk.

To his astonishment, instead of gold he saw a pile
of gingerbread cakes! Each one had the king's
head stamped on it, just like a coin. He raged
and swore – but he had given Bill a receipt for his
rent, so there was nothing he could do. Everyone
would laugh at him if people heard the story of
how Bill had got the better of him.

The New House

The children were very excited when they heard that they were going to move to a new house. Now that the twins were getting bigger, there didn't seem to be enough room in the cottage for all the family. The children were delighted to hear that their Granny would be coming to live in their old home.

"That means that we will see her every day," said Ronan. The children loved their Granny and they especially loved to hear her stories.

"And what's more, we will have stories every day," said Sinéad, hugging her brother.

The family were very pleased with the plans for the new house. Everyone looked forward with great excitement to the day when the building would start and the twins began to plan how they would decorate their own room.

One day Granny came to visit. The children told her of their plans and all was well until Granny asked where the new house was to be built.

"It's to be at the top of the field near the cottage," replied Ronan.

Granny didn't seem pleased to hear this.

"It is a beautiful place to build a house, isn't it?" said Sinéad. "We will be able to see the sea from the door and we will be able to visit you every day. Why aren't you happy, Granny?"

Granny hurried to speak to the children's father.

"Eamon," she said, "you can't build your new house at the top of that field. The fairy people

live there. No one must ever disturb those bushes in any way. Cut a single branch and you will never again have any luck!"

Eamon just laughed.

"That's only an old story. No one believes stories like that any more!"

He refused to listen to her. The building began. Every day the children rushed home to see what had been built. Every night they talked and planned excitedly, but they noticed that Granny never joined in the conversations.

On the day the family moved into the new house, Eamon invited his friends and neighbours to a big party to celebrate. Most people were delighted to accept, but some of the older people of the village thanked him and made excuses not to come.

The party was held on a beautiful summer's evening. There was plenty to eat and to drink. Eamon had organised musicians and both young and old joined in the dancing.

At midnight, a breeze began to stir and soon it got stronger and colder until it became a howling wind. The sky grew darker with huge black clouds. Suddenly, strange hammering noises came from inside the roof!

One by one the guests left. By now the noises were much louder and they seemed to come from everywhere – the roof, walls and chimney. The children were terrified.

"It's the fairies and leprechauns!" they cried.

Granny was right.

"We must go quickly, right now!" she cried.
Eamon was the last to leave. He looked back and
gasped! He could hear leprechauns hammering
and smashing!

The house shuddered and collapsed. Then the little people disappeared in a swirl of leaves.

Eamon and his family lived for many years in their little cottage. No one ever dared to touch the pile of bricks that had been their new house. After a time, the site became overgrown with hawthorn bushes and the land belonged once again to the fairy people.

Oisín in Tír na n-Óg

One morning the Fianna were hunting deer on the shores of Loch Léin in Kerry. They saw a beautiful white horse coming towards them. Riding on the horse was the most beautiful woman they had ever seen. She wore a long dress as blue as the summer sky, studded with silver stars, and her long golden hair hung to her waist.

"What is your name and what land have you come from?" asked Fionn, Leader of the Fianna.

"I am Niamh of the golden hair. My father is king of Tír na n-Óg," she replied.

"I have heard of a warrior called Oisín. I have heard of his courage and of his poetry. I have come to find him and take him back with me to Tír na n-Óg."

Oisín was the son of Fionn. He was a great hero and a poet.

"Tell me," Oisín asked Niamh, "what sort of a land is Tír na n-Óg?"

"Tír na n-Óg is the land of youth," replied Niamh.

"It is a happy place, with no pain or sorrow. Any wish you make comes true and no one grows old there. If you come with me you will find out all this is true."

Oisín mounted the white horse and said goodbye to his father and friends. He promised he would return soon. The horse galloped off over the water, moving as swiftly as a shadow. The Fianna were sad to see their hero go, but Fionn reminded them of Oisín's promise to return soon.

The king and queen of Tír na n-Óg welcomed Oisín and held a great feast in his honour. It was indeed a wonderful land, just as Niamh had said. He hunted and feasted and at night he told stories of Fionn and the Fianna and of their lives in Ireland. Oisín had never felt as happy as he did with Niamh and before long they were married.

Time passed quickly and although he was very happy, Oisín began to think of returning home for a visit. Niamh didn't want him to go, but at last she agreed, saying:

"Take my white horse. It will carry you safely to Ireland and back. Whatever happens you must not get off the horse and touch the soil of Ireland. If you do this you will never again return to me or to Tír na n-Óg."

She did not tell him that although he thought he'd only been away a few years, he had really been there three hundred years.

Ireland seemed a strange place to Oisín when he arrived back. There seemed to be no trace of his father or the rest of the Fianna. The people he saw seemed small and weak to him.

As he passed through Gleann na Smól he
saw some men trying to move a large stone.

"I will help you," said Oisín.

The men were terrified of this giant on a white
horse. Stooping from his saddle, Oisín lifted
the stone with one hand and hurled it. With
that the saddle girth broke and Oisín was flung
to the ground.

The moment Oisín tumbled to the ground the white horse disappeared and the people saw before them an old, old man with long white hair and a beard.

As Oisín sat on a rock, recovering his senses, he remembered Niamh's words to him before leaving Tír na n-Óg: on no account was he to touch the soil of Ireland or he would never again return to his beloved.

The people of Gleann na Smól gathered around the old man. Unsure of what to do or how to help him, they took him to see a holy man who lived nearby to seek his advice.

"Where is my father and the Fianna?" Oisín asked. When he was told that they were long dead he was heartbroken. He spoke of the many deeds of Fionn and the Fianna and their adventures together. He spoke of his time in Tír na n-Óg and his beautiful wife that he would not see again. Although he died soon after, the wonderful stories of Oisín have lived on.

The *Sidhe*

Once upon a time, a man called Séan lived in a small cottage near a small village. During the long winter nights the people of the village used to meet and tell stories or sing to pass the time.

Séan loved the music and the stories, but unlike his family and neighbours, he didn't believe in fairies or leprechauns or any of the little people. In fact, whenever he heard anyone talk about the Sidhe he would laugh and say that he couldn't understand how anyone could be so foolish as to believe that such stories could possibly be true.

One warm summer day, Séan was resting by the edge of his field. The air was filled with various sounds. He heard birds chirping and busy bees humming as they collected pollen.

Suddenly, he became aware of another sound. It was a gentle tap-tapping which seemed to come from a nearby hedge. Séan moved forward slowly to investigate.

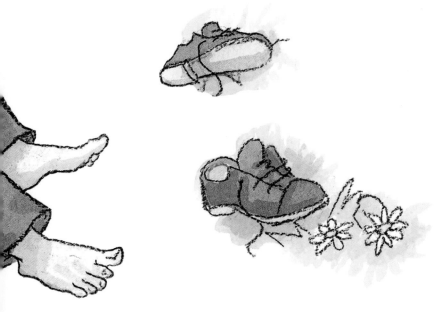

He couldn't believe what he saw before him! It was a real live leprechaun, exactly like those that Séan said didn't exist. The little man was there in front of him, sitting on a mushroom working hard. At his feet lay many different pairs of shoes, some with silver buckles, some dainty fairy slippers and some boots.

In a flash, Séan reached out and grabbed the little man.

"Where is your pot of gold?" he demanded.

"Gold!" said the little man crossly. "Gold! Where would I get a pot of gold? I'm only a poor shoemaker. All I have are my tools and this piece of leather."

"You can't fool me," said Séan.

"Give me your gold and I'll set you free."

"All right!" the little man cried.

"My gold is buried safely in the field by the river. Take me there and I'll show you."

From the stories he had heard, Séan
knew exactly what he had to do to get the
leprechaun to part with his gold. He must
not take his eyes off the man for an instant.

The leprechaun led him to a bush near the
water's edge, in the next field.

"There you are," he cried. "Take my gold."

Keeping his eyes on the leprechaun,
Séan reached into the bush. Suddenly
he gave a scream of pain, for instead of
a pot of gold he had put his hand
into a bee hive!

Of course he looked to see where the bees were.
As soon as Séan had taken his eyes off him, the little
man vanished, just as the stories said he would.

Séan never told anyone how the leprechaun had fooled him when it was his turn to tell a story during the long, cold winter nights.

But no-one ever again heard him say that he didn't believe in fairies or leprechauns.

Saint Patrick

Patrick stood on the deck of a boat as it rolled up and down in the swell of the sea. He peered into the misty distance and caught sight of the shore. Patrick was returning to Ireland, the country where he had been sent as a slave when he was just 16 years old.

He had escaped from harsh slavery as a young
man and, after many travels and adventures,
had settled in France where he became a priest.
There he had a dream, telling him to return to
Ireland and take God's message to the people.

Patrick watched as the sailors skilfully guided the
boat in between jagged rocks, and in a moment
he heard the scrape of pebbles against the bottom
of the boat. He pulled his rough woollen robes up
around his waist and jumped ashore. The sailors
called goodbye and turned the tiny boat around,
out to sea. Patrick stood on the beach. His mission
to convert the pagan Druid people of Ireland
to Christianity was about to begin.

Soon, Patrick heard that Laoghaire, the High King of Tara, had summoned all the chiefs of Ireland to a feast. The Druids were about to celebrate the coming of spring with a special ceremony. The High King ordered that all fires and lights in all the surrounding lands were to be put out until a great fire was lit on the royal Hill of Tara.

This pagan festival was to take place at the same time as the Christian celebration of Easter. Patrick decided to show the pagan people the power of Christianity. He and his followers met at the Hill of Slane, at the opposite end of the valley to the Hill of Tara. There they lit their own huge fire and it blazed high into the sky.

The Druids were very angry when they saw this. They thought Patrick wished to be stronger than the High King of Tara. They told the king that if he was to keep his power over the people, he must defeat Patrick. So they ordered their fire on the Hill of Tara to be lit and soon the whole valley was aglow from the fires at each end. It was a spectacular sight that men would talk about for many years to come.

The king, his soldiers and the Druids marched across the valley to Slane. They tried in vain to put out Patrick's huge fire. They even tried to kill Patrick but he stood bravely in front of the fire, singing hymns and praising God. The fire burned through the night and its light shone across the land. The king saw that Patrick was not to be defeated by force, and it made him think perhaps, after all, the Druids did not have all the answers.

The next day, King Laoghaire invited Patrick
to come to Tara and tell him about Christianity.

On his way to Tara, Patrick stopped by the
roadside to pick a bunch of shamrock, a plant
that was sacred to the Druids; he tucked it
into his robes.

The king listened to all that Patrick had to say about God and the Gospels and the beliefs of the Christian faith.

Some of it was very difficult to understand, especially the Christian belief in the Trinity: how could God actually be three people, the Father, the Son and the Holy Ghost?

Suddenly Patrick had an idea. He pulled out the bunch of shamrock and broke off one leaf. There were the three petals on the one stem, three in one – just like the Trinity!

The king understood Christianity that day and he realised that Patrick did not want to be more powerful than him. Once the king saw that Patrick was not in competition with him, he agreed to give him permission to preach the Gospel throughout the land.

And so it was that Patrick came back to Ireland in peace and with the message of God. He tirelessly travelled the land, spreading the word and establishing the Christian faith.

Eventually he became the patron saint of Ireland, and the shamrock became the national emblem.

Oisín

It was evening and Fionn was returning home. His two hounds Bran and Sceolán were at his side.

Suddenly, a fawn jumped out in front of them and immediately the hounds gave chase. Fionn followed and, to his great surprise, when he finally caught up with them, the hounds were lying peacefully beside the fawn.

"She must be one of the Fairy people," he thought to himself.

During the night Fionn woke to find a beautiful young girl standing at his bedside. He knew that she must be the fawn he had hunted that day.

"I need your help, Fionn," she whispered softly.

"My name is Sadhb, and you are the only one who can help me. Two years ago, one of the druids of my people, the Fear Dorcha, wanted me to be his wife. When I refused, he cast a spell on me and turned me into a fawn. Only the man I love can protect me."

"Tell me where he is and I will take you to him," Fionn answered.

"He is here in front of me," cried Sadhb.

"While I am with you I can take human form and the Fear Dorcha cannot harm me."

Fionn was delighted to hear this, for he had fallen in love with Sadhb as soon as he had seen her.

Within a short time they were married and they lived happily in his fort on the Hill of Allen.

One day Fionn received news that the Norsemen were coming again, in their longships, to attack. Fionn made preparations to leave at once. It was the duty of the Fianna to protect the country from any invaders.

Before leaving he warned Sadhb not to venture outside the fort until he returned. The fight was long and difficult, but eventually the invaders were driven back to their ships. Immediately, Fionn set off for home.

As Fionn approached the fort he became troubled. He could see no sign of Sadhb coming to greet him. Then he grew fearful and rushed into the fort. His chief steward came to him and told him terrible news.

"One morning as Sadhb looked over the plain, she gave a great shout of joy. She cried out that you were returning. We looked out and we saw you with Bran and Sceolán, but were surprised that none of your warriors was with you. Before anyone could say a word, Sadhb ran out to welcome you home."

"As she drew near you, she realised that it wasn't you, but the Fear Dorcha. We were powerless, and could only watch helplessly as he touched her with a hazel rod and she

became a fawn. She tried to escape but
his two hounds prevented her. There
was nothing we could do!"

Fionn spent the next seven years searching for Sadhb, but with no success. One evening, as he was returning home, his two hounds suddenly raced off in the direction of a small wood. Fionn was overcome by a strange feeling, and followed them curiously.

There, under a tree, was a little boy of about seven years old. The boy and Fionn looked at each other. Then the little boy reached out his hand and placed it in Fionn's. Fionn looked into the boy's face and recognised the eyes of his beautiful wife, Sadhb. He knew that this was his son.

The little boy returned home with Fionn. At first he could not speak, but gradually, as he learnt the language, he told Fionn about the fawn that had taken care of him.

He spoke about a tall, dark man who would appear and try to talk to the fawn, but she would always run away. The last thing he remembered before meeting Fionn, was the dark man hitting the fawn with a hazel rod and forcing her to follow him.

"You are indeed my son," said Fionn sadly.

"I loved your mother, but the Fear Dorcha stole her away from me. He has no power over you. You will stay with me and when you are old enough you will join the Fianna. I will call you Oisín, Little Fawn."

Oisín became a very great warrior and a famous poet. When he grew up he visited his mother in Tír na n-Óg.

The **Magic Cloak**

I t was almost dawn. Both sea and land were covered in mist. Eoin hid behind the rock as the tide ebbed far out into the bay. He had been waiting a long time for this special day. Every seven years a very strange magical event happened.

The old people in the village said that the sea
went out as far as the horizon and the fairy people
appeared. They spread a magic cloak in the centre
of the sands and this held back the tide. Whoever
owned the cloak could order the sea to stay back
and would have good fertile land to make a farm.

Eoin always listened carefully to the stories
the old people told, especially this one. Seven
years earlier, he had crept out and watched in
amazement as the waves rolled back and the
fairy people appeared! This time he waited with
his horse tethered nearby. At dawn they came.
Eoin could hear the music of the fiddles and
harps. Through the mist he could barely make
out the shadows.

Slowly he got on his horse, making sure not to
startle the animal. The mist lifted and once again
Eoin saw the strangest sight before his eyes. The
sea and sand had disappeared and in its place
was a green plain as far as he could see.

Eoin knew what to do. He had to get the magic cloak – and the land would be his! But the cloak was guarded by leprechauns. He soon spotted them sitting in a circle, a pile of tiny shoes at their feet, tapping in time to the music. They were sitting on the cloak and the edges were flapping in the breeze.

Eoin pulled gently on the reins of his horse as they moved forwards. It took him longer than he expected to reach the cloak. When he looked back, it seemed that the shoreline was very far away in the distance.

As he came near to the leprechauns he slowed his horse and then dismounted a short distance away. He crept forward. He thought that they must hear his heart thumping or the sound of his breathing but no, they continued to work.

He reached out and, taking hold of a corner of the cloak, he pulled it from under them. Without delay he threw the cloak on his back, mounted his

horse and galloped towards
the shore. He could hear
the chaos and confusion
behind him but he dared
not look back.

Suddenly all was quiet. It was an eerie quiet. The breeze dropped.

"I've made it!" Eoin thought.

Then he heard a rumbling noise. He looked over his shoulder and moving towards him with terrific speed was a gigantic wave. It was the Fairy Wave!

Eoin urged his horse on but he was swept from the saddle. He felt as if he was being pulled in many directions and beaten by many pairs of hands.

As quickly as it had come the wave disappeared. When Eoin woke and tried to move, every bone and muscle in his body ached.

"I've survived the Fairy Wave," he thought.

"I have the magic cloak. I can control the sea and I'll be rich. I have beaten the fairies. I don't mind the pain."

He put his hand on his back to feel the cloak but instead all he felt was a cloak of seaweed.

Lazy Annie and her *Amazing Aunts*

Annie was very beautiful. She was also the laziest girl in Ireland! One day a prince rode by her house.

"Surely you aren't scolding that lovely girl?" he asked when he heard her mother giving out. The old woman was ashamed to admit how lazy Annie was.

"My daughter works too hard! She can spin, weave and make the cloth into shirts within three days."

"My mother is the best spinner in the land," said the prince. "I'd like to take Annie home with me and introduce her to the queen!"

The old woman didn't want to admit that she had
been untruthful about Annie's skill at spinning
and weaving, so she agreed that her daughter
should go. Annie was delighted to be invited to
the prince's home. She sat on his horse, and they
rode away together.

On the journey, Annie and the prince fell in love.
They planned to marry – but Annie didn't dare
confess that she couldn't spin, or weave, or sew!
What was she to do?

When they reached the castle, the queen welcomed Annie. She could see how beautiful Annie was but she was even more pleased to hear that she was such a hard worker.

That night, Annie found a huge pile of flax on her bedroom floor.

"Start first thing in the morning," the queen told her.

"I'll look forward to seeing the thread the day after tomorrow. Goodnight!"

And with that, the queen left Annie alone in the bedroom staring forlornly at the pile of flax.

The next morning, Annie started to cry because she couldn't spin. Suddenly, a funny old woman with very big feet appeared!

"Why are you crying?" she asked Annie.

"I have to spin all this by tomorrow, and I don't know how to do it," Annie sobbed.

"Leave it to me," the old woman said.
"Ask Colliach Cushmor to your wedding,
and the thread will be ready tomorrow."

"Of course I'll invite you," Annie said.
"You'll be very welcome."

By morning all the flax had been spun into
the finest thread. The queen was delighted.
"Excellent!" she said.

"Tomorrow you can weave that into cloth
on my own loom. Have it done by evening."

Annie was very frightened. She had no idea how
to use a loom! She was sitting beside it sobbing
when an old woman with huge hips appeared.

"I'm Colliach Cromanmor," she announced.
"Invite me to your wedding, and I'll weave
that thread by tonight!"

"Please come!" Annie said. And so the old woman started work. That evening, the queen ran the cloth through her hands.

"How soft and delicate!" she exclaimed. "Make it into shirts tomorrow and my son will wear one at your wedding!"

Early next morning, Annie sat sorrowfully by the cloth. She feared she would lose her prince, for she had no idea how to sew!

It was midday when a third old woman arrived.She had an enormous red nose! She introduced herself as Colliach Shrón Mór Rua, and asked for a wedding invitation.

"I'd be delighted if you came," Annie told her.

By nightfall, the old woman had made twelve perfect shirts.

After a magnificent wedding, there was a splendid banquet. Suddenly a footman announced: "Princess Annie's aunt, Colliach Cushmor!" The old woman with big feet came in. The prince's mother thought the old woman looked strange.

"Why are your feet so big?" she asked rudely. "Because I've stood spinning all my life," Colliach Cushmor told her.

"Annie, you must never spin again," cried the prince. The footman called out again:

"Princess Annie's aunt, Colliach Cromanmor!" In came the old woman with huge hips. The queen stared.

"Why are your hips so huge?" she demanded.

"Because I've sat at a loom all my life," the old woman answered.

"Darling, you must never weave again," the prince told Annie. Again the footman called:

"Princess Annie's aunt, Colliach Shrón Mór Rua!" The old woman with the red nose approached. "Why is your nose red?" demanded the queen. "Bent over my sewing every day, all my blood ran into my nose," the old woman replied.

"Dearest, never sew!" cried the prince.

So, thanks to these three old fairies, Annie knew she need never spin, or weave, or sew, but could live for ever as an idle princess!

Children of Lir

Once upon a time there lived a king called Lir who had four children: a daughter named Fionnuala and three sons called Aodh, Fiachra and Con.

Their mother the queen was dead, and the children missed her terribly. They missed the stories she used to tell them, the games she used to play, and the songs she sang at bedtime as she hugged them to sleep.

The king saw that his children were sad and needed a mother, so he decided to marry again. His new bride was called Aoife. She was beautiful, but she was not the kind-hearted person the king thought she was.

Aoife grew jealous of the four children because their father loved them so much. She wanted the king all to herself, so she planned to get rid of the children. She asked a druid to help her, and together they thought up a terrible spell.

In the castle grounds there was a large lake which the children loved to play beside. One day Aoife went with the children to the lakeside. As they played in the water, she suddenly pulled out a magic wand and waved it over them. There was a flash of light, and the children vanished. In their place were four beautiful white swans.

One of the swans opened its beak and spoke with Fionnuala's voice:

"Oh, what have you done to us?" she asked, in a frightened voice.

"I have put a spell on you," replied Aoife.

"Now everything you have will be mine. You will be swans for nine hundred years. You will spend three hundred years on this lake, three hundred years on the Sea of Moyle and three hundred years on the Isle of Glora. Only the sound of a church bell can break the spell."

When the children did not come home that evening, the king went back to look for them by the lake. As he came near, four swans swam up to him. He was amazed when they began to call out.

"Father, Father," they cried, "we are your children. Aoife has placed a terrible magic spell on us."

The king ran back to the castle and pleaded with Aoife to change the swans back into children, but she refused. Now he saw how selfish she was and banished her from the kingdom. Lir promised a reward to anyone who could break the spell, but nobody knew how.

Lir spent the rest of his life beside the lake, talking to his children, until he grew old and died. The swans were heartbroken. They no longer talked or sang, and nobody came to see them.

Three hundred years passed and it was time for the swans to move to the cold and stormy Sea of Moyle between Ireland and Scotland.

The poor swans were tossed about by the wild waves and dashed against sharp rocks.

It was a harsh life with little food and the years passed slowly.

When the time came for them to fly to the Isle of Glora, the swans were old and tired. Although it was warmer on the island and there was lots of food, they were still very lonely.

Then one day they heard the sound they had waited nine hundred years for. It was the sound of a church bell.

The bell was ringing in the tower of a little church. An old man, called Caomhóg, stood outside. He was amazed to hear swans talking and listened to their sad story in astonishment. Then he went inside his church and brought out some holy water which he sprinkled on the swans while he prayed. As soon as the water touched them, the swans miraculously began to change into an old, old woman and three old, old men.

Lir's children were frightened. Caomhóg told them about God and his love for all people. They no longer felt scared. Fionnuala put her arms around her brothers and all four old people fell to the ground, dead.

Caomhóg buried them in one grave. That night he dreamed he saw four swans flying up through the clouds and he knew that the children of Lir were at last on their way to Heaven to be with their mother and father again.

Pronunciation Guide

Ailill
Al-ill

Ainle
Awn-la

Aodh
A

Aoife
Ee-fa

Binn Éadair
Bin Ay-dir

Bran and Sceolán
Bran and Sk-oh-lawn

Brian Borumha
Brian Brr-um-ha

Brodir
Bro-deer

Caoilte Mac Rómáin
Queell-te Mock Row-mawn

Caomhóg
Quee-vogue

Cennetig
Ken-ay-tig

Cluricaune
Clur-e-cawn

Colliach Cromanmor
Coll-i-ock
Cro-man-moor

Colliach Cushmor
Coll-i-ock Cush-moor

Colliach Shrón Mór Rua
Coll-i-ock Sharone
Moor Ru-a

Conán Maol
Con-awn Mw-ayl

Connacht
Con-ock-t

Cooley
Coo-lee

Coomara
Coo-ma-ra

Cú Chulainn
Cu Cul-in

Cumhall
Coo-all

Daire Mac Fiachra
Da-ra Mock Fee-ack-ra

Dal Cais
Dal Gash

Donal an Clogaidh
Do-nal On Clog-a

Eamon
A-mon

Eimer
E-mur

Eisirt
Esh-irt

Eithne
Eth-na

Eoin
Owe-en

Fear Dorcha
Far Dr-aka

Feidhlim
Fay-limb

Fiachra
Fee-ack-ra

Fianna
Fee-a-na

Finnbhennach
Fin-van-ock

Finnéigeas
Fin-e-gas

Fionnuala
Fun-ew-la

Gleann na Smól
Glawn Na Small

Grainne Mhaol
Grawn-yeah Wheel

Granuaile
Grawn-yeah Whale

Hill of Howth
Hill of Hoath

Laoghaire
Lee-ar-re

Leabharcham
La-ow-er-cam

Lios
Lis

Loch Lein
Lock Lane

Lough Neagh
Lock Nay

Maelmordha
Male-more-ah

Maeve
May-v

Mahon
Ma-hun

Malachy
Mal-a-key

Naoise
Ne-shah

Niamh
Ne-a-of

Oisín
Ush-een

Phouka
Foo-ka

Sadhb
Sigh-v

Samhain
Sau-in

Sinéad
Shin-aid

Sliabh Bloom
Sleeve Bloom

The Sidhe
The Side

Tír na n-Óg
Tier ne Nogue

Uisneach
Ish-knock

Una
Oo-na

Index